Thomas James MacMurray

The Legend of Delaware Valley

And other Poems

Thomas James MacMurray

The Legend of Delaware Valley
And other Poems

ISBN/EAN: 9783744770576

Printed in Europe, USA, Canada, Australia, Japan

Cover: Foto ©Andreas Hilbeck / pixelio.de

More available books at **www.hansebooks.com**

" The youth sought out the monarch's tent
To sue for that proud sire's consent
To union with the lovely maid
    Who was the idol of his heart ;
But, heedless of the pleas he made,
    The stern chief told him to depart."

—*See page* 10.

THE

LEGEND OF DELAWARE VALLEY,

AND OTHER POEMS.

BY

REV. THOMAS J. MACMURRAY, LL.B.

———————

TORONTO:

WILLIAM BRIGGS, 78 AND 80 KING STREET EAST.

1877.

Dedication.

TO THE WIFE OF MY YOUTH.

Cherished companion of my life,
   Your love, unchanged through changing years,
Has e'en grown stronger in the strife,
   And triumphed over doubts and fears.

When other faces blanched with dread,
   When other hearts grew sick and faint,
You still pressed on, though hopes were dead,
   Nor paused to utter one complaint.

As the lone rock for aye abides,
   Though beaten by the angry wave,
So you have stemmed opposing tides
   With heart the bravest of the brave.

Your steadfast love and sympathy,
   Your admonition, kind and good,
Betoken inward purity
   And noble, queenly womanhood.

Beloved, accept this book of song—
   This simple wreath of poesy;
And may your words, so sweet and strong,
   Still guide, sustain and comfort me.

CONTENTS.

———◄►—◄►———

vi

CONTENTS.

CONTENTS.

The Legend of Delaware Valley,

AND OTHER POEMS.

—◦◦❬❭◦◦—

The Legend of Delaware Valley.

[The superstition regarding the fatal consequences of killing a white deer is of Indian origin. The Indians believed that a white deer was sacred and possessed a charmed life. From ancient Indian times has been handed down the following interesting legend, which the pioneer settlers in the Delaware Valley solemnly related, and which is still told by credulous inhabitants of the Lackawaxen region]:

I.

FAR back in dim, primeval days,
    As this strange Indian legend says,
    There dwelt upon the Delaware
An Indian princess, wondrous fair;
And many of her dusky race
Admired the beauty of her face,
Her flowing hair, her lustrous eyes,
Her mien that never knew disguise,

2

Her voice that, like an angel's lute,
Rose soft at night when birds were mute.

II.

Her father's tribe was brave and strong,
Whose prowess was the theme of song.
One in that tribe—a valiant knight,
The brave in many an Indian fight—
Loved the proud chieftain's only child ;
And ofttimes through the forest wild
The youth sought out the monarch's tent
To sue for that proud sire's consent
To union with the lovely maid
   Who was the idol of his heart;
But, heedless of the pleas he made,
   The stern chief told him to depart.

III.

More popular and brave became
The Indian youth, and far his fame
Went out among his noble race,
And the chief's rage increased apace.
The flame of envy in him burned,
For the young hero he had spurned
Had won, by chivalry, a name
Far prouder than the chieftain's fame.

The tribe sang of his deeds so brave;
To him they costly presents gave;
And maids danced for him round the fire
To war-songs that rose higher, higher,
Till from the home of birch and oak,
And from the swamp, wild echoes broke.

IV.

At length the chief conceived a plan
To rid him of the dreaded man;
So, sending for the warrior bold,
The crafty Indian ruler told
The youth he could the princess win
If he would drive an arrow in
The body of a snow-white hart,
And slay it with his cruel dart,
Then lay at the red monarch's feet
The body of the deer so fleet.

V.

The Indian lover read his doom
And wandered to his lonely home,
For never had a marksman's art
Sent arrow through a white deer's heart.
But the proud chief called in once more
The warrior whom he hated sore.

He also called the sorcerer,
  Whose suit the princess had just spurned,
  And the magician's anger burned,
And he had sworn revenge on her :
He placed within the lover's hand
A stalk that was a magic wand ;
'Twas silver-tipped, and long, and clear,
" And none but it can pierce the deer
Whose life is guarded by a charm,"
Spoke out the sorcerer, to harm.

VI.

Now the young warrior left the chief,
And to his breast had come relief ;
The arrow, silver-tipped, would find
The snow-white deer of rarest kind ;
And he would shoulder it with pride,
And claim his own—his royal bride.
Thus hoping, he dashed through the wood,
Till by a crystal lake he stood
O'erlooking Lackawaxen vale,
And there he watched the hunter's trail.
Tall cedars fringed the placid lake,
And here the deer came out to take
A cooling drink and then march back
Along their old, familiar track,
Through cedar brush and hemlock boughs,
Then in some nook lie down and drowse.

VII.

When shadows of the evening fell
O'er silver lake and stream and dell,
The Indian lover's birch canoe
Shot out from where the lilies grew.
Now everything was still as death ;
Nor was there in the air a breath
To break the stillness so profound
That reigned supremely all around.
The hunter's mind was anxious now ;
His eye glanced on the mountain's brow,
Then at the cedar copse near by,
Where shadows deepened silently.
Once more the lonely hunter gazed,
And now his splendid bow was raised ;
A herd of deer stole from the wood
And knee-deep in the water stood,
And one of them was white as snow.
Now leaped that arrow from its bow,
And, gleaming in the twilight air,
Went crashing through the white deer's hair—
Ay, even through its very heart
Leaped the young warrior's fatal dart.

VIII.

The white deer fell, its wild death-cry,
Reverberating far and nigh ;

But while that cry resounded still
About the lake and forest hill,
The young brave's arms lost all their strength,
The power of speech left him at length,
And o'er that lake so still and bright
He drifted, drifted day and night,
With parchèd tongue and wasted frame,
And never any succor came.
Nor did his sufferings abate
Till death drew near and sealed his fate.
Two summer moons had come and gone
Ere human eye had fallen on
The Indian warrior, brave and true—
That skeleton in birch canoe.

IX.

The shooting of that fatal dart
Into the sacred white deer's heart
Brought to the warrior untold grief,
And to the jealous Indian chief
It brought calamity as great;
For when the lover met his fate,
At sunset of that fatal day
On which he shot his shaft away,
The great chief fell upon his bed,
And when they saw him he was dead.
An arrow in his heart was found,
And blood was oozing from the wound.

X.

The Indian princess, thus bereft
Of parent and of lover, left
The wigwam and sought out the lake—
The silent haunt of hern and crake—
Where died her lover true and brave,
And in its depths she found a grave.
Then in that happy Spirit-land
She clasped her faithful lover's hand;
And still through forests grand they walk—
He armed with bow and tomahawk;
She decked in garments of a queen,
Her face lit up with smiles serene.

XI.

The sorcerer, avenged at last,
Now saw the tribe of stately caste—
The tribe once powerful and grand,
That conquered every hostile band—
Weakened and crushed by sore defeat,
And lying at a conqueror's feet.
No more its battle-songs were sung;
No more were its bright banners flung
Upon the breeze. The tribe went down,
And with it fell its fair renown.

XII.

And now old settlers softly tread
The shores of White Deer Lake.   They dread
To make such noises as might wake
The slumb'ring Spirits of the lake;
And oft they pause with bated breath
To view that dismal lake of death.
And folk along the Delaware
Still gather in the fireside glare
To hear this Indian legend told,
And speak of the young warrior bold
Who buried the magician's dart
Into the sacred white deer's heart.

Regret.

TO-NIGHT I chide myself, for my loved friend
    Has passed away from earth and sensuous life,
    And I am conscious that I did not lend
Him aid enough in his terrestrial strife.

How frequently it lay within my power
    To make his gloomy pathway smooth and bright,
By telling him, in sorrow's lonely hour,
    Such words as would have given him true delight!

I could have been more thoughtful and more kind
    When he was ill, and faint, and sore distressed;
I could have comforted his heart and mind,
    And brought him hours of sweet content and rest.

What rare benevolence I might have shown
    My noble friend in all those vanished years!
Alas! too late—too long did I postpone
    My sacred task, and bitter are my tears.

For my departed friend will not return
    To bless me with his sympathy again;
And on my lips regretful words now burn,
    While in my heart dwell loneliness and pain.

La Republique.

READ ON THE OCCASION OF A FOURTH OF JULY CELEBRATION.

THE nation **exults in** her freedom to-day,
　　Her glorious flag proudly waves in the wind,
　　While over the ocean and far **o'er** each bay,
There goes forth **a song** from the millions **combined.**

'Tis the song of our **Freedom the** multitudes sing—
　　The song of releasement **from** despotic reign;
And the triumphal notes in melody ring,
　　Till o'er the whole land we **can** hear the refrain.

A free, grand Republic, **a hundred** years old,
　　'Tis the **first on** the earth in splendor and fame;
And tyrants who wrought 'mong **us suff'rings** untold,
　　Have **learned** to respect her **proud,** honored name.

We boast of the heroes who fought for our flag,
　　And carried it high through the bloodiest strife,
To plant it, with shouts, over turret and **crag,**
　　While each **of** the enemy fled **for** his life.

Let us visit the graves of our soldier dead,
  And deck them with flowers that are sweetest and
    rare ;
For those were the heroes who fought and who bled
  To give us this free land, whose blessings we share.

The contest has ended ; the morning has come ;
  Peace now sits enthroned as the queen of our
    realm ;
No tocsin of war, no alarm of the drum,
  Does now our gigantic nation o'erwhelm.

Here industry prospers on every side—
  From the North to the South, and from sea to sea ;
And the shout of the millions goes far and wide :
  "Hurrah for the Union—the home of the free !"

Here genius and learning hold conquering sway ;
  Here brains, and not rank, must insure our success ;
And poor, honest peasants, who toil day by day,
  Are never despised on account of their dress.

May our motive of life be "Good-will to men" ;
  Our watchword be "Onward!" our motto "Reform!"
May no angry war-cloud sweep o'er us again,
  To smite our fair nation with darkness and storm.

May happiness reign in the homes of our land,
　　And virtue adorn both the young and the old ;
May treason, so foul, nevermore lift its hand
　　To rob us of freedom more precious than gold.

Hoist the stars and the stripes in Liberty's name !
　　Sing the song of sweet freedom with spirit and
　　　　power,
While every heart is with zeal all aflame,
　　And each pulse is throbbing with joy at this hour.

Come patriots all and take part in the strain
　　That echoes in gladness o'er land and o'er sea !
To the brave, honored dead pay tribute again,
　　And sing of a nation forever made free.

The Sailor's Child.

A MOURNFUL wind crept o'er the hill,
The sun had sunk, and birds were still,
And sadly plashed the solemn sea
Against the rocks below the lea.

Bare was the bosom of the deep
That stretched afar from rocky steep;
No white sail gleamed from out the haze,
Nor moon nor star shot forth its rays.

Far out upon the ocean wild
A sailor dreamed of wife and child;
He saw his cottage in the trees;
He heard sweet songs and childish glees.

How heaved his heart, at morn, with love!
No longer did he want to rove;
Then from his eyes tears fell like rain,—
The sailor sighed for home again.

Eight summers had his daughter seen,
And to that father she had been
Just as an angel pure and white—
His sweet companion day and night.

'Twas June when she was called away
Into the light of endless day,
To bloom within yon heavenly sphere,
Far from the pain and sorrow here.

For June, it was a dismal night;
Portentous clouds shut out the light
Of silver moon and twinkling star,
And waves moaned on the harbor bar.

Eva heard for a month and more
Those waters dashing on the shore,
While in her silent room she lay,
Her fair form wasting fast away.

Her little boat lay on the beach,
Its shattered hull the waves did reach,
And as it rocked with every swell,
The ocean tolled its funeral knell.

" Mother," she said, as death drew near,
" Father's out in a gale, I fear:
Do you not hear the ocean's roar?
How loud it sounds upon the shore!

" I see a white sail through the spray;
The ship comes fast into the bay;
'Tis father dear!   O let me stand
Beside the sea and wave my hand!"

Eva left as the clock struck three ;
She now rests where there's no more sea !
Her grave is in the yew-tree's shade,
Beneath whose boughs she often played.

The sailor's ship came home at last,
When autumn's glowing red was cast
Upon the wooded slopes around,
And leaves were covering the ground.

No bounding feet the father heard,
No childish voice his feelings stirred,
As up the garden walk he sped ;—
Eva was numbered with the dead.

But ever and anon he hears
A gentle voice of other years ;
Nor can he hush that haunting tone
That makes his heart more sad and lone.

Henry Wadsworth Longfellow.

IN MEMORIAM.

HE has gone from the land where his songs ever
 ring,—
  From the shore of Time's sea,
  From the world and from me;
He has sped to the Isles of perpetual Spring,
To take part in the chant which the bright angels sing;
  And the Poet's sweet spirit is free.

For his country he sang in the loftiest strains;
  How he chanted its woes!
  How he vanquished its foes
When they cruelly tried to bind Freedom with chains,
To inflict on the helpless the losses and pains
  That tyranny only bestows!

In the picturesque hamlet—in palace and hall—
  In the cot rude and lone,
  His sweet verses are known,
To the rich and the lowly, the great and the small;
And the Poet is honoured and loved by them all,
  For that brotherly love he has shown.

O Bard of our country! we pause at thy tomb,
　　To let fall one fond tear
　　On those flowers that appear
Above thy still form that inhabits the gloom;
But thy songs, like the fragrance of flow'rets in bloom,
　　Shall delight us for many a year.

The Old and the New.

I.

THE grand old year has passed away!
　　Its joys have also flown;
　　And now, obscured by twilight gray,
While round my cot the cold winds play,—
　　I muse while all alone.

There come to me, in clusters rare,
　　Mem'ries—now bright, now sad—
Of pleasant walks and faces fair,
And happy hours when preying care
　　Did flee, to make me glad.

The clam'rous rill, and lonely grot,
　　And fairy midnight scene,—
These were my joy when 'twas my lot
To rest where Nature's beauties dot
　　The spot with matchless sheen.

3

But, ah! with the departed year
   Have gone those pleasures sweet,
And down my cheek there flows a tear,
For past scenes will not re-appear—
   Save in the mind—to greet.

As flies the swallow to her nest,
   As dies the dream at morn,
So years, obeying the behest
Of nature, pass away to rest
   'Mid quietude forlorn.

Farewell! thou dying year, farewell!
   In splendor thou hast shone!
Adieu, past hours! List to the knell
Of the loud-sounding chapel bell
   That says, "The year has gone!"

II.

The bells now ring—with a startling din—
The Old Year out and the New Year in;
And people are thronging the city street,
Going to and fro on rapid feet,
And everywhere there is kindly greeting,
For face to face warm friends are meeting.

The bells chime out with a wild ding, dong,
Filling the frosty air with a song

Of welcome glad to the fair New Year
That comes to us with the brightest cheer;
And now the world's great pulse is bounding,
And homes with music are resounding.

The bells clang out with clarion voice,
And a million hearts do now rejoice,
And faces are wreathed with sunny smiles
In this midnight hour that so beguiles,
While chapel bells are gaily ringing
To festal sounds of mirth and singing

The Poet's Song.

WHEN thou hearest music stealing
    Near thee, to arouse thy feeling,
        Wilt thou then think of me?
For I sang a humble sonnet
To thy heart, and quickly won it:
    Shall that song stay with thee?

When in distant lands thou rovest,
Far apart from those thou lovest,
    Pray, wilt thou think of me,
And recall our first fond meeting,
And each blissful after greeting?
    Shall my song comfort thee?

When thy friends shall speak thy praises,
Bring thee flowers in costly vases,
  And crave thy company,
Will thy heart forsooth be glowing
With a love that, ever growing,
  Giveth its wealth to me?

Bereft.

WHERE is my little one sleeping to-night?
    Who watches over her bed?
    What tender lullaby closed her blue eyes,
  After the daylight had fled?
Will she be guarded from danger and harm?
  Will her eyes nevermore weep?
Tell me, O tell me, ye angels above,
  Where does my little one sleep?

What does she dream on that strange, distant shore,
  Where mists like a phantom play,
And fair isles rest in a motionless sea
  That throws not a chilling spray?
O sweet be thy sleep, my departed child!
  May thy dream-visions be bright!
Though I cannot see thy angelic face,
  I'm thinking of thee to-night.

Soon I shall pass to that beauteous shore,
  Whither my darling has crossed ;
Soon I shall clasp to my bosom again
  The one that is loved and lost ;
Then shall I know where she peacefully slept,
  And who the bright spirits were
That kept nightly vigils over the couch
  Where rested my darling fair.

Manhood.

BE wise to-day. Folly drags down
    Its votaries to vice and shame ;
    But wisdom gives to man a crown
  Of honor and-a noble name.

Let justice guide thee every hour ;
  Nor let one narrow prejudice
Rob thee of moral worth and power
  And fill thy soul with selfishness.

Be tender and affectionate
  In all thy intercourse with men ;
Harbor no jealousy nor hate,
  Nor manifest a proud disdain.

Look up in faith to God above,
　In recognition of His care,
And thank Him for His boundless love
　That comes to soothe thee everywhere.

So, having wisdom, justice, love,
　And simple faith in the unseen,
Thou shalt in manhood's beauty move,
　With heavenward gaze and lofty mien.

The Robin.

ONE summer in the long ago,
　A robin daily sang to me
　His love-song, full of melody,
That cheered my heart and soothed my woe.

Then came December's blast so weird,
　Yet my wee bird flew not away,
　But staid to sing in winter's day,
Tho' all his mates had disappeared.

I fed him at my window-sill
　So tenderly each early morn,
　And pitied him: he looked forlorn,
With no bird near on forest hill.

Each day he sang his happy song,
  Nor seemed to care for blinding snow,
  Or threat'ning clouds that brooded low,
Or piercing gales that swept along.

Ere I arose his notes I heard
  Ring out upon the wintry air,
  And thought it strange indeed to hear
That sweet song of my lone, lone bird.

But one fell day my Robin flew
  Not down from out his leafless tree
  To eat the crumbs, and sing to me,
And cheer my life when fierce winds blew.

Beneath the oak tree by the door
  I found my Robin in the snow—
  The bird whose sweet notes charmed me so
In melancholy days before.

Ah! dear, dead bird! I'll ne'er forget
  The winter song I heard thee sing,
  And those bright hours that thou didst bring;
I fancy now I hear thee yet.

O, blessed be the merry voice
  That in the wintry days of pain
  Brings to the ear some sweet, loved strain
That makes the pensive heart rejoice.

Vivere sat Vincere.

WE need not dread the closing hour,
   If we have grandly won the day;
   Death welcomes home the chieftain brave
From toil, and care, and madd'ning fray.

Honors await each noble knight
  Who climbs life's rugged precipice,
Nor ever falters on the rocks,
  In terror of some dark abyss.

Life's duty done and journey o'er,
  We can lie down at evening's close,
Expectant of the honors rare
  That kind, indulgent heaven bestows.

"To conquer is to live enough;"
  Ah, yes!   And gladly would we greet
The tranquil eventide of life,
  Were we prepared its close to meet.

But there are tears to wipe away,
  And we must cheer the fretted heart
In its deep loneliness and woe,
  Ere we would willingly depart.

The fight 'gainst wrong has just begun,
 Nor would we throw our armor down
Till freedom's banner was unfurled
 And we had won the victor's crown.

Fight on, fight on, O manly soul!
 And though thy road be dark and rough,
Ne'er falter in thy heavenward course;
 "To conquer is to live enough."

The First Snow.

THE first snow falls on the frozen ground;
 Gently it falleth—without a sound—
 On the withered leaves and faded grass;
And my heart is heavy as I pass
Along the way where my feet erst trod
In days when the early golden-rod
Fringed the bank of the crystalline stream,
And when life seemed like a summer dream.

The first snow falls on my weary heart,
And my first grief makes the tear-drops start;
My cherished hopes have gone to decay,
As flowers of the woodland fade away

When touched by November's chilly breath;
For now she lies in the arms of death—
Yes, the one I loved so long ago
Is sleeping to-day beneath the snow.

The first snow falls on her lonely grave
That nestles where weeping willows wave;
And wintry winds, as they hasten by,
Seem to sing a plaintive lullaby;
For the lovely things of earth are lost—
All buried in graves of snow and frost;
And some day, how soon I do not know,
I, too, shall be lying 'neath the snow.

The Song of Home.

A SWEET strain trembles in every air,
    And floats o'er each crystal sea :
     'Tis the song of home—oft sung in prayer
When wafted to you and me.

The sire who treads on some foreign shore,
    Sings of home and children dear ;
And his sad strains mingle with the roar
    Of wild waters far and near.

At nightfall when the fisherman skips
    Over the billows that foam,
There's but one am'rous song on his lips,
    And that is the song of home.

That song is raised by peasants at eve,
    When the long day's work is done ;
And loved ones haste the kiss to receive
    At the setting of the sun.

Forgot are songs that merrily rang ;
    Hushed are the voices so sweet ;
But the song of home our mothers sang,
    Still floats, every ear to greet.

Though it draw a tear, come, raise that song
   Of the dear old home we love !
And when on earth we have sung it long,
   We'll sing of sweet home above.

Our Fallen Heroes.

DRAW near to the graves of our heroes
   With gentle and reverent tread ;
     Bring flowerets—affection's sweet tokens—
And scatter them over the dead.

How bright their achievements of valor !
   How loyal their sentiments were !
Then bring wreaths of loveliest blossoms
   For heroes whom war did not spare.

Tread softly among the May grasses
   That over the graves gently wave ;
The heroic dead are here buried—
   The loyal, the noble and brave.

They now sweetly rest after battle ;
   Their long weary marches are done ;
No more shall they suffer or sorrow,
   Or faint under heat of the sun.

Come now with fair blossoms of May-time,
  And scatter them over each grave
In which sleeps a soldier and hero
  Who died the Republic to save.

Of the Past.

, HOW the heart longs for the days that are past,
  And yearns for the loved gone before !
  How often we sigh, when our sky is o'ercast,
And wish for a rest and a calm that would last
  Thro' the years—ay, last evermore !

As mem'ry flies back over each bygone year
  To the spot where our treasures are laid,
We sigh to hear voices and songs that are dear,
And the harp that poured out its harmony clear
  Where sweet, smiling infancy played.

How delightful to hear, like an evening chime,
  The voices we heard long ago !
They come floating adown the river of Time
With an echo so sweet and a tone sublime,
  As the sound-waves ebb and flow.

And our fancy sees, on a strange, fairy shore,
  White hands that now beckon us there ;
And the love-whispers, soft and sweet as of yore,
Now are borne through the mists to our ears once more
  From that country of purer air.

O, 'tis sweet to know, when the stars fade from sight,
  And the roses of June decay,
That memory cheers us in sorrow's drear night,
And that hope sheds over our pathway its light,
  And foretells of a coming day.

Tho' the summers go, and the violets fade,
  And loved ones depart to the bourn,
We may live in the past, with memory's aid,
And recall the bygone, with its shine and shade,
  And 'tis sweet, e'en if we must mourn.

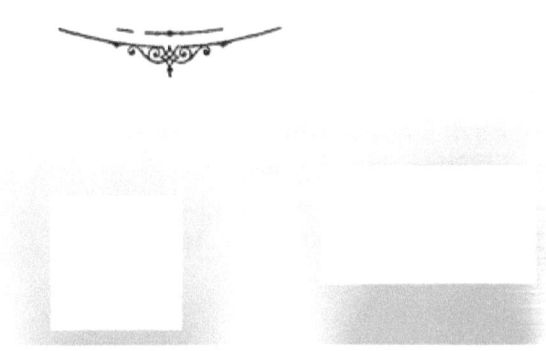

Trusting.

LET my way be bright or gloomy
   As I journey here,
     I can always feel contented
With my Saviour near.

He has promised He will guide me
   All along life's way;
He will show me love and pity
   When I faint or stray.

In the bygone years I've tested
   His unbounded love;
Nor do I now fear to trust Him
   As I onward move.

Shall I doubt Him, then, when sorrow
   Comes into my heart?
Dare I say He does not love me,
   When the tear-drops start.

O, no other loves so fondly !
  He is my best friend ;
From the first He loved me, and will
  Love me to the end.

Then I'll go into the future
  With a courage strong ;
Though the road be rough and thorny,
  It will not be long.

Soon the glad, refulgent morning
  Shall bring in the day,
And the undertone of sadness
  Soon will die away.

Then a song shall burst in gladness
  On my list'ning ear,
And my heart, once lone and heavy,
  Shall be filled with cheer.

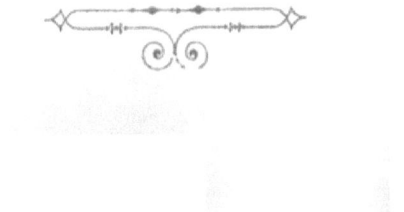

The Farmer's Wife.

DON'T give me the life of a farmer's wife,
   Its drudgery and its care,
     Its weary routine from morning till e'en,
  With never a moment to spare ;
For who, I would ask, would covet the task,
  Of rising before it is day,
The breakfast to get and the table to set,
  All to hustle the men away !

Don't talk of the breeze in the summer trees,
  Or the swallow's delightful song,
Or places that charm on the dear old farm,
  Or the labor that makes one strong :
For the dreary life of a farmer's wife
  Is never by these things blest ;
No hour has she to stroll over the lea
  In search of a much-needed rest.

Through the weary years she labors in tears,
  While her heart is loving and true ;
" Each day is too brief," she remarks with grief
  "To accomplish all there's to do."

So she toils with might till on in the night,
    And is up ahead of the sun;
The " men folks" repose at the long day's close;
    But her labors are never done!

A Dream.

A N old man sits in his easy chair
    On a dreary winter night,
      His face as white as his flowing hair
  That shines in the lamp's dim light.

And he falls asleep to dream at last
    Of the happy days of yore,
While anon the smould'ring embers cast
    A glare on the oaken floor.

O, wake not the peaceful dreamer now,
    Before his dreaming is done;
No shadow rests on his wrinkled brow;
    Then let his wild fancy run.

In dreams he now lives in other days
    When his heart throbbed not with pain;
O'er his father's fields he once more strays,
    And he romps as a child again.

He sees his home in the quiet wood,
  Beside the murmuring sea,
And stands on the beach where oft he stood
  Ere he left his native lea.

He sees the majestic ships go by,
  As in long, long years before,
And hears again the sea-bird's cry
  And the wave's plash on the shore.

He hears the voices of long ago,
  And the songs that charmed his youth;
He watches the log-fire's ruddy glow,
  And listens to tales of truth.

The old man smiles in that fair dreamland,
  For he sees a face so dear;
He feels the touch of a mother's hand,
  And the dreamer drops a tear.

Beautiful dream of that aged man!
  O, that it might last for aye!
So bright are youth's scenes to him again;
  Do stay, happy vision—stay!

*   *   *   *   *   *   *

The embers faded; the hearth grew cold;
  Yet the sleeper moved not his head;
His spirit had flown through the gates of gold—
  The pale-faced dreamer was dead.

A Portrait.

LINES WRITTEN ON RECEIVING MY MOTHER'S PICTURE.

I CANNOT describe her endearing, calm face
   That glows with such infinite beauty and grace,
   Revealing the deepest affection and thought
Through those wrinkles that time and sorrow have
  wrought.

The wealth of her love never fails through the years;
It is always the same, through smiles and through
  tears;
Though other hearts wither and friendships grow cold,
Her heart aye beats for me with love that's untold.

Bright summers depart, and sweet violets fade,
And death sweeps o'er meadows in verdure arrayed;
But amid all decay, and change, and unrest,
Burns the flame of true love in a mother's breast.

I gaze on this portrait with fondness and pride,
As a lover would look on his lovely bride;
But an image more lasting dwells in my soul
Of her who will love me while cycles shall roll.

Infinite Tenderness.

WHENE'ER the soul is crushed with bitter grief,
And every fondly-cherished hope has flown,
Who but the Comforter can give relief,
Or turn to joyous song life's minor tone?

So insufficient is mere human speech
To soothe the spirit in its dire distress,
That we almost unconsciously do reach,
With trembling hand, for God to come and bless.

Compared with His alleviating grace,
How weak the sympathy of mortal men!
He takes the suffering world in His embrace,
Nor holds it near His tender heart in vain.

When break affliction's waves against the soul,
When fades from human ken hope's cheering star,
Come Thou, O Mighty Guide! and take control
Of the frail bark that drifts with tides afar.

Though tempests rage, and sorrow's night be drear,
And no bright beacon-light points out the land,
The trusting voyager need never fear,
While sheltered in the hollow of His hand.

Longing.

COME back, ye birds that far have flown;
    I long to hear your songs again;
    I'm weary of the bleak wind's moan,
The falling snow and pelting rain.

Return, ye sunny days I love;
    My life is cheerless now and cold;
The heavy, threat'ning clouds above
    My head unceasingly have rolled.

I cannot longer bear to look
    On snow-clad hill and wintry waste,
Or on those sad woods birds forsook
    In bitter sorrow and in haste.

My rose-bush has been bare so long!
    And how I wish the May's sweet breath
Would come and scatter life among
    The stems where now there's only death!

E'en now my heart with hope is filled;
    For soon the merry birds will come;
And gentle rains will be distilled
    O'er flower-beds rich with sweet perfume.

Earnestness.

BE earnest in this life; be true;
    And whatsoe'er thou hast to do,
    Perform it with thy zeal and might,
For soon will come death's solemn night.

Success depends on earnest work;
The men who daily duties shirk
Are cowards who will never rise;
For such there is no victor's prize.

Only the earnest, noble, brave,
Who battle with each wind and wave,
Nor ever heed misfortune's frown,
Attain the heights of fair renown.

This is no dreamland where we may
Slumber and dream the years away;
But 'tis the scene of active life—
The battle-field—the school of strife!

Here the contestants rise or fall,
They soar in thought, or else they crawl;
But earnest souls, whose hearts are pure,
Shall rise, and their reward is sure.

Be earnest, then, for time is brief,
And broken hearts sigh for relief;
Work zealously while shines the sun,
If thou would'st hear the words " Well done!"

Song.

1.

I AM sitting in the twilight,
    And I dream of long ago,
        When the mild voice of my mother
    Spoke to me so sweet and low ;
I can see the home I cherish,
    And can hear the brooklet's song
Down beside my father's orchard,
    Where I wandered oft and long.

        Linger still, fond dream of childhood;
            Do not vanish yet, I pray !
        For the darkness creeps upon me,
            And my home is far away.

2.

Fancy sees the forms of dear ones
  That I loved in other years;
But those forms have all departed,
  And mine eyes are wet with tears;
O, the sadness that steals o'er me
  While I dream of childhood's hours,
And the scenes of youth so blissful—
  Scenes of love, and joy, and flow'rs!

3.

Now the old house is deserted,
  And the place is lone and drear,
And I'll never hear the music
  That allured my youthful ear;
And the wrinkled hands that labored
  To illumine all my way,
Nevermore will toil or suffer
  Thro' the long and weary day.

A Simile.

THE air is chill, and autumn grieves
  O'er withered flowers and falling leaves ;
    The time has come when glories fade
In garden, mead and wooded glade,
And when sweet birds, that carolled long,
Must sing to us a farewell song.

My life is in the leaflet sear ;
The chill winds of old age I hear ;
Spring's morn has fled ; the summer's gone ;
My cheeks are furrowed now and wan ;
No more rings out youth's mystic chime ;
My life has reached the autumn time !

The Indian's Grave.

I FOUND it on a forest hill,
   That overlooked a glassy lake ;
    Around the mound tall grass and brake
Had spread their soft and showy frill.

I stood as in the sight of death,
   Nor dared to break the hush profound,
    Or wake the sleeper under ground ;
And so I paused with bated breath.

Scarce moved the ferns between the rocks
   That rose like gravestones near the dead ;
    Scarce shook the branches overhead,
That oft had reel'd with sudden shocks.

A slender cross lay on the grave ;
   An Indian maid had placed it there,
    And forest flow'rs, of beauty rare,
To her lost love she daily gave.

No more in red canoe he'll skim
   In sport across the placid lake ;
    No more adown the stream he'll take
The lovely Indian girl with him.

He will not roam thro' swamp again,
  Nor chase old bruin from his log,
  Nor saunter forth with gun and dog
To hunt the wild buck on the plain.

The hills will echo nevermore
  With his wild song or rifle-shot;
  Ah, me! the maid whose heart he got
Must sail alone by that lake shore!

And often when the night-shades fall,
  The maid steals thro' the forest grim
  To sit beside the grave of him
Who answers not her plaintive call.

Ofttimes she sits on moss-clad stone
  To watch the sleeping, moon-lit sea;
  And while she listens eagerly,
She seems to hear a low, low moan.

Is it the water's mournful lay
  That falls upon her list'ning ear?
  Or only distant echoes drear
That issue from the dying day?

No; 'tis the voice of her lost love
  That echoes thro' the snow-white mist,
  And o'er that lake, by moonbeams kiss'd,
A white canoe is seen to move.

So every night the Indian maid
  Can see that white canoe near by,
  Gliding along so silently
Past rocky shore and wooded glade.

She's true to him thro' all the years;
  None else could she in truth adore,
  For love is love for evermore—
In joy, in pain, through smiles and tears.

She mourns a loss forever new;
  And by that grave she'll daily weep,
  And nightly vigils she will keep
To see her lover's white canoe.

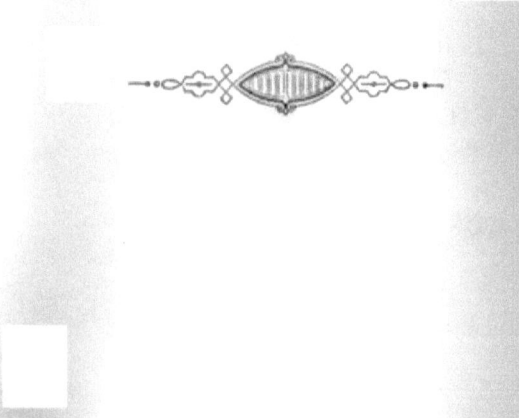

Witnessing for Christ.

" Ye are my witnesses."

I'LL witness for Jesus,
  Whatever befall,
    And speak of the anguish
  He bore for us all.

Why should I be silent,
  When Love brought Him down
That I might be given
  A robe and a crown?

Ashamed to confess Him
  Who loves even me?
Ashamed of my Saviour
  Who died on the tree?

O, no! I will herald
  His greatness each day,
And deem it an honor
  This homage to pay.

Should darkness o'ertake me
  On life's raging tide,
I'll trustingly witness
  For Jesus, my Guide.

And when I step into
  The river of death,
His name would I mention,
  E'en with my last breath.

Thus if I prove faithful
  And true to the end,
I'll not be rejected
  By my Divine Friend.

Some Day.

SOME day we shall lay down the burdens of life
    That we have been bearing with patience for
       years;
Some day we shall rest at the close of the strife
    And rejoice after all our mourning and fears.

Some day we shall enter the mansions above
    To commune with dear ones whom death took away;
And there in the light of our kind Father's love
    We shall joyously chant thro' eternal day.

Some day we shall know all the mysteries deep
    Of that Providence oft so strangely revealed—
Know why in this earth-life God called us to weep
    And to suffer the wounds that still are unhealed.

Some day we shall wonder at Heaven's expanse,
    Its long, gorgeous aisles, and its throne grand and
    . white,
Its glittering hosts, and its songs that entrance;
    And our eyes shall scarce bear the marvellous sight.

No tears will be shed on that evergreen shore ;
  No sighs will break out 'mong the glad, dazzling
    throng ;
But bliss unalloyed will reign **evermore**
  On those hills that echo with rapturous song.

At Rest.

SEPTEMBER winds were sighing through the
    vale,
  And glowing tints bedecked the woodland fair,
When one with furrowed brow and features pale
  Lay down to sleep ; for she was **worn** with care.

'Twas fitting that when **earth's** delightful things—
  The grasses, leaves and **flowerets** bright and gay—
Were perishing, her spirit should take wings
  And fly to realms where flowers fade not away.

But oh ! I had no truer friend than she—
  No wiser counsellor—no safer guide !
The home I loved is nothing now to me,
  Bereft of her in whom I could confide.

  5

Nor could I bear to view that lonely place ;
   The sight would call up mem'ries sad and deep ;
And only fancy could behold her face
   Or hear her song that oft soothed me to sleep.

Let autumn winds wail out their sad refrain ;
   Let flaunting, golden flowers now fade and die ;
I too must grieve amid my loss and pain ;
   Yet hope's lone star shines dimly in my sky.

Those hands that toiled so long are resting now ;
   That gentle voice is hushed at last, at last ;
The fever and the pain have left her brow ;
   All toil is done—all agony is past.

Farewell, old home !   I'll visit thee no more !
   Farewell, the haunts I loved in other years ;
Farewell, thou limpid stream, upon whose shore
   I played, before my eyes grew dim with tears !

March.

THE blustering March has come again—
The hated month of all the train,
  When bleak winds rush with mighty roar
Along the lake's deserted shore.

A dreaded month! yet it will bring
The glories of returning Spring,
And help to place, with right good-will,
The floral crown on every hill.

The broken clouds pass swiftly by,
In haste to clear the azure sky;
And rills, long ice-bound, now are free
To leap in gladness toward the sea.

Soon will the grateful scent of flowers,
Wafted from aromatic bowers,
Invite us to the sylvan vale,
Our languid spirits to regale.

The fitful blasts that sweep along
Shall bear to us Spring's charming song,
And birds, that come with breezes bland,
Shall warble in our northern land.

Then, March, I gladly welcome thee,
For thou art a true friend to me;
And though thy winds and frowns annoy,
These are but harbingers of joy.

Loneliness.

AS comes a stillness to the festive halls
    When jocund banqueters have gone,
        So steals o'er me a feeling that appalls—
A loneliness when day is done;
For happy scenes I knew in days of yore
    Come nevermore to gladden me;
The old, delightful songs I hear no more;
    Hushed is the merry minstrelsy.

In other years I thought the world was bright
    And everybody in it true;
Each day I lived was one of mirth; each night
    Was filled with song that sweeter grew.
Alas! the scene has changed. The friends I loved
    And trusted proved untrue, unkind;
And haunts, once pleasing, where my footsteps moved,
    I have no more desire to find.

Alone I live.   Ambition's dreams are dead ;
  My feet are weary on life's way ;
Shut out from all the world—my hopes all fled—
  I but exist from day to day.
My roses faded in the years long past ;
  Only their thorns are left with me ;
And yet, despite the cares that shadows cast,
  My heart has one fond memory :—

It comes like music o'er a sleeping sea
  And comforts like an angel's psalm ;
Down through the years it floats so peacefully
  And fills my lonely soul with calm ;
It brings before my vision once again
  A face observed through mists and tears,
And maybe in that country, free from pain,
  We'll meet and love through endless years.

The Lost Grave.

[About ten years ago the Detroit *Free Press* commented on a touching incident which occurred in that city, and which is substantially as follows :—An old woman was seen wandering through the deserted graveyard on Russell Street. She had buried a child there half a century before, and in all those years she had not seen the little grave; but her undying love for her child brought her clear back across the State alone to have a last look at the grave. She found the old yard cut up by streets, and of the hundreds of mounds and headstones which she once saw, but a score or so were left. Under the dying willows she passed along, brushing the moss from the headstones, and trying to find the stone which bore the words, "Our Willie." Her search was fruitless. She had hoped that strangers' hands might have kept the grave as when she last saw it, and she turned sadly away from the barren spot, the tears falling on her wrinkled cheek ; and when the people spoke to her in sympathy, she sobbed out, " I'm afraid I can't find him in Heaven —Heaven's so large ! " This sad incident suggested the following lines] :—

THEY saw her wand'ring in a graveyard old ;
　　They heard her sobbings in the willows' shade,
　　And well they knew her heart desired to hold
Some sweet communion with her sacred dead.

Full fifty years had passed since she had seen
　　The spot where rested Willie's lifeless form ;
And yet her love, thro' every changing scene,
　　Was as a mother's love,—unchanged and warm !

But she had hoped, thro' every lonely year,
  That grave might not be slighted or forgot,
But that some passing stranger, kind and dear,
  Would cast on it a sweet forget-me-not.

She hoped some one might scatter daisy seeds
  In springtime o'er her Willie's little mound,
And for the absent dead do loving deeds
  When autumn leaves were covering the ground.

Alas! she found the old yard almost gone,
  For fifty years had made a cruel change,
And only here and there she saw a stone,
  While all the scene to her was new and strange.

The town had grown to be a city grand;
  The sacred charms of long ago had fled
Before Time's hostile and o'erpowering hand,
  And those who lived were crowding out the dead.

But that old mother's heart had brought her back
  To view that grave ere she had passed away,
And shed on it affection's tear, and deck
  It gently o'er with flowerets bright and gay.

'Mong leaning headstones, covered o'er with moss,
  She sought the grave she had not seen for years;
But after walking to and fro across
  The barren fields, she then gave way to tears.

Ah, me ! that mother came alone so far,
    With burdened, anxious heart and features wan ;
But from her sight had sunk hope's last faint star,
    For Willie's little grave was lost and gone !

Kind words were spoke to her by passers-by,
    Who saw the tears fall on her wrinkled cheek ;
Her tale of woe aroused a sympathy
    Too strong for any human tongue to speak.

And while she stood beneath the dying trees,
    Once more to view the fields so bleak and lone,
Her sobs went out on every passing breeze,
    As she remembered glories that had flown.

She left the scene, nor e'er returned again ;
    Her heart was broken with her bitter grief ;
She tarried thro' a few more years of pain,
    Then Death's kind angel brought her sweet relief.

And as she swept thro' Heaven's gates of gold
    Into the brightness of that glorious place,
That mother's heart beat with a joy untold
    When her own Willie ran to her embrace.

The Absent.

HOW lonely seems each weary day
    Without thy presence near!
    Upon my path no cheering ray
Shines through the darkness drear.

I miss thy voice so sweet and low,
    Thy prepossessing face,
Thine eyes, whose fascinating glow
    Now haunts me every place.

Ah, me! We know not how to prize
    The sunshine and the flow'rs
Till they are gone and wintry skies
    Frown on the faded bow'rs.

We value not the robin's song
    Till it has closed its strain;
And then our lonely spirits long
    To hear that song again.

Nor do we fully prize the friends
  In whom we can confide,
Till our communion with them ends,
  And they have left our side.

Back o'er the years agone we gaze,
  We see the loved of yore,
While gentle songs of other days
  Float from an unknown shore.

And so to-night I dream and weep;
  The midnight comes apace,
But brings not to my eye-lids sleep,
  Nor to my sight thy face.

Sonnet to Friendship.

LIFE'S journey is not very long;
  Earth's pleasures are seldom too sweet;
  So let us have laughter and song,
And kind words whenever we meet.
The roses sweet perfume exhale;
The sunshine sheds gladness around;
And the brooklet down in the dale
Makes woodlands with music resound.
The nightingale heeds not the gloom,
But charmingly sings in the night,
Its song waking thoughts from their tomb,
And filling the soul with delight.
The face that we gaze on to-day
May to-morrow be pallid and cold;
Then scatter bright smiles on the way,
To gladden the young and the old.
When the light of friendship is shed
O'er a life embittered by pain,
The sad heart that often has bled
Is cheered and made hopeful again.

The Road to Success.

IF you want to succeed in this life,
　　You must have an abundance of pluck;
　　There is no one can win in the strife
By relying on what is termed "luck."
Temptations must be bravely withstood;
　　Even poverty must be o'erthrown;
And, with purposes lofty and good,
　　You must struggle and suffer alone.

Be content to toil on through each year,
　　Yielding not to one idle desire,
Till the goal of your hopes shall appear
　　And your deadliest foes shall retire.
Do not fancy the road to success
　　Is bestrewn with the loveliest flowers;
All along it are thorns that distress,
　　And the pilgrim sees few sunny hours.

Every day brings the toiler some pain,
　　While each evening brings weariness, too;
But continuous efforts bring gain
　　To the one who finds something to do.

Learn to work and to patiently wait ;
   Learn to calmly endure each defeat ;
And some day you'll sit down with the great
   Who have won a reward doubly sweet.

Lines,

SUGGESTED BY THE AUTHOR'S VISIT TO TOM MOORE'S COTTAGE
ON THE SCHUYLKILL RIVER.

, SACRED and enchanting spot !
   Where now it is my happy lot
   To linger one brief hour and rest,
And list to Nature's voices blest ;
Here, on the Schuylkill's flow'ry shore,
I muse on Erin's bard, Tom Moore,
Who often sang of this fair scene,
In verse so cheerful and serene,
And drew an inspiration deep
From stream, and wood, and blooming steep.

   No poet sang in sweeter strain ;
Whether he wrote of joy or pain,
His every verse, so rich and free,
Was fraught with wondrous melody.

His country's harp was silent long;
But from its chords he drew a song
Whose music, magical and grand,
Reverberates in every land,
Although the harpist sleeps in death,
Nor heareth now that music's breath.

I wonder not the poet loved
This charming spot, and often roved,
At eventide, this flow'ry bank,
To watch the red sun as it sank
Behind the dim and distant hill,
And hear the latest song-bird's trill,
And listen to the muffled oar
On river's breast, or the dull roar
Of the great city so near by
That pulsates on unceasingly.

A Memory.

'VE waited long to hear his step again—
　　Waited through weary years of grief and pain,
　　For his familiar footfall at the door
From which he vanished many years before,
When the June rose exhaled its sweet perfume,
And every hill was decked in gorgeous bloom.

I've waited long to hear his pleasing voice,
Whose welcome music made my heart rejoice ;
And in the years when he was far away
I ofttimes seemed to hear his blithesome lay,
As when we sat beside the summer sea
While evening shadows gathered o'er the lea.

I've waited long to see his manly face
Beam light into my lone and gloomy place,
As morning's dawn dispels the shadows drear
That through the long night linger everywhere.
Alas! 'tis but my fancy that can see
The noble face that used to smile on me !

My hair, once golden, is now turning gray;
My beauty and my youth have passed away;
Those hopes are blasted that I prized for years,
And now I walk alone the vale of tears,
With but a memory—a beauteous dream
To throw athwart my path its friendly gleam.

The years have sped!　And now it matters not
Though that long-absent one I fondly sought
Return to me no more from o'er the sea,
To keep the solemn vow he made to me:
He may be happy at another's side;
Or long, long years ago he may have died.

Were I but sure he loved me even now,
The cloud of sadness would desert my brow,
And I could go down life's decline in peace,
And all my dread anxiety would cease,
If I could only know his love was true—
Unchangeable as heaven's resplendent blue.

Perchance 'twas best that we should meet no more
In lovely bower, or by the sad sea shore;
Yet when I now recall the happy past—
The golden hours of joy that could not last,
Sad tears stream down my pale and faded cheek,
And thoughts arise no tongue can ever speak.

May Song.

AROUND me the gentle May zephyrs are playing;
   They waft to me perfumes · from florulent
    bowers;
And over the bright fields I once more am straying,
  While peace fills my heart thro' the long, sunny
   hours.
The robin's sweet notes and the meadow-lark's sonnet
  Fill all the soft air from morning till eve;
And the shimmering sea, with the sun shining on it,
  Invites the gay bark its bright waters to cleave.

So weary I grew of the bleak, wintry weather—
  The frost and the snow that staid with us so long!
But to-day my heart is as light as a feather,
  As I listen to Nature's most jubilant song.
The bee hums its way to the fields of sweet clover,
  The lambs now skip playfully over the lea,
And along by the sea-shore wanders the plover,
  While birds build their nests in each blossoming tree.
  6

How bright is the world! and how green are the
    meadows!
  Nor trembles a minor strain in the soft air.
Can it be that over this scene will fall shadows,
  And that chill frosts will come to blast what is fair?
Think not of what may be! 'Twill bring only weeping!
  Shall birds warble gladly and we never sing?
With the brightness of May grief is not in keeping,
  Then sing of the pleasures a May-day can bring.

Kindness.

SELDOM does a kindness go for naught;
    Somewhere, sometime we shall see
    What results our kindly deeds have wrought
  In relieving misery.

Humble was the song you sang one day
  To delight some listener's ear;
But you little thought your tender lay
  Gave fresh hope to mourners near.

Simple was the loving word you said;
  But that word came from the heart,
And it wakened feelings that were dead,
  And caused tears of joy to start.

It was but a smile that you bestowed—
  Just a smile and nothing more;
Yet a heart with gladness overflowed
  At the look your features wore.

Thus it is that kindness is not lost:
  Gen'rous deeds and words of cheer,
Smiles and songs—all help the tempest-tossed
  To be hopeful strugglers here.

The Poet.

ALONE he sits among his books;
    Nor does he toil in vain;
      Deep thoughts are written on his looks,
  Grand problems fill his brain.

His neighbors call him a recluse,
  And think him cold and queer;
They say he is of little use
  To anybody here.

But in his room, the noble sage,
  Regardless of their hate,
Toils daily o'er the open page,
  From early morn till late.

THE POET.

The years go by.   Now every voice
   Speaks in the poet's praise ;
Behold, the multitudes rejoice
   To hear his simple lays.

For touchingly he sang their woes
   In verse sublime and pure ;
The years roll by, yet sweeter grows
   The song that shall endure.

Its melody awakens joy
   Within the pilgrim's breast ;
And when his earthly cares annoy,
   It calms his wild unrest.

O, white-haired bard, sing on, nor cease
   To quiet human fears !
Thine is the power to fill with peace
   The realm of pain and tears.

Envy.

THE world is selfish, in the main;
  One rises to a fair renown
 By manly toil of hand or brain;
 Then others try to drag him down.

Envy detests the laurels bright
  It cannot wear, and loves to hate
The victor who has reached the height
  Of excellence, in spite of fate.

As savage wolves hunt down the deer
  That, panting, bounds thro' wilderness,
So envy, with its with'ring sneer,
  Pursues the man who wins success.

Some will rejoice with those who rise;
  But more will look with envious eye
On such as win the costly prize;—
  The world is full of jealousy.

O, envious man! why strive to crush
  Thy brother and to blast his name?
Thou hast an equal chance to push
  Thyself to fortune and to fame.

Hope.

THROUGH life's chequered scenes we are borne
  By a stern, irresistible power,
    While our hearts are saddened and torn
With the woes that come hour after hour.

When no one but God knows our fear,
  We lie down by the wayside to weep,
And though we are weary with care,
  Our sad eyes will not close in sweet sleep.

But hope! There are joys with our woes;
  Ay, the dark clouds are fringèd with light;
We have friends to drive back our foes;
  There is sunshine alternate with night.

Though forms that we love pass away,
  And we oft sit alone with our tears,
Yet fond mem'ries frequently stray
  Through the dim, lengthened vista of years.

Our Father is near when we grieve,
  All our sorrows He soothes with His grace;
To Thee, loving Saviour, we cleave;
  We can sing in the light of Thy face.

By the Sea.

, ROLLING sea! Thou tell'st a tale
    That makes my cheek grow deathly pale.

Sad, lovely sea! With thee I weep;
And on thy breast I fain would sleep.

The night is chill, the wind is bleak;
Far out I hear the sea-bird shriek.

My footsteps press the hardened sand
That marks the bound of sea and land.

Over the dim, dark wave I gaze,
And think of other, happier days.

I long to touch a hand so white,
That vanished from me in the night,

And catch the music of a voice
Whose tones once made my heart rejoice.

O, plaintive night-wind, bleak and lone,
I cannot bear to hear thee moan!

Thy sobs recall the by-gone years
And melt my weary eyes to tears.

O loved and lost ! come back once more
And greet me on this ocean shore.

Speak to me, as in days gone by,
Nor leave me here to sink and sigh.

I listen, but no voice comes near
From out the darkness dense and drear.

The moaning of the restless sea
Is all the sound that floats to me.

My lonely heart cries out in vain ;
The lost will ne'er come back again.

Sob on, O sea ! Sigh on, O wind !
Ye seem so heartless and unkind !

Nor shall I longer with you stay ;
The midnight bids me haste away.

But none, O ever-rolling sea,
Can comprehend thy mystery !

A Summer Night.

NOW sinks the sun into the restless sea;
  The purple glow on hill-top fades away;
  Grim shadows gather softly o'er the lea,
And gently closes the long summer day.

The crescent moon sails up the star-lit sky,
  Shedding on wave and slope her silver light;
And 'mong the tree-tops the soft breezes sigh,
  As if in dread of the approaching night.

No longer sings the robin or the lark,
  Whose mellow notes were heard in sunny hours;
But nestling in the woody covert dark,
  They wait the light that gladdens all the bowers.

Naught but the watch-dog's bark, or cricket's song,
  Or ocean's murmur, falls upon the ear,
And the dull hours drag heavily along,
  While strange, weird shadows come and disappear.

The moon-lit waves plash faintly on the shore,
　　Where sombre cliffs lift high their tow'ring forms,
So heedless of the sea's incessant roar—
　　So firm against the oft-recurring storms.

Long clouds of vapor spread their fleecy folds
　　Athwart the lowlands robed in summer bloom,
And faintly outlined are the open wolds
　　That look like fairy-haunts amid the gloom.

O'er this night-scene what solemn silence reigns !
　　Nor bird nor bee disturbs the dreamy air ;
And drooping flowers now seem to miss the strains
　　That joyous day diffuses everywhere.

Autumn Winds.

SAD autumn winds! I hear your wail
 That echoes through the sombre vale
 And speaks of days, not far away,
When birds shall cease their roundelay
And flowerets shall not longer shed
Their fragrance o'er the hills I tread.

O, autumn winds! Your chilling breath
Shall usher in decay and death,
And maple groves that now are bright
Shall sigh amid the autumn blight,
And meadows shall grow brown and bare
And ruin meet me everywhere.

Chill autumn winds! Why do ye come
To rob the maple of its bloom,
And take from me the things I love?
Ah me! the things we prize above
All else are sure to fade and die,
E'en though we love them tenderly!

O, blighting winds! Ye come to bring
Death to the cheek that blushed in spring!
Life's summer o'er, the autumn blast
Destroys the bloom that could not last;
Then groweth dim the tearful eye,
And, like the flowers, we droop and die.

Life's autumn days I will not fear!
For, as the flowers again appear
When o'er the earth blow zephyrs bland,
So, when I reach that fairer land,
Where spring-time's sun shall ever shine,
Immortal Youth will then be mine!

Separation.

SLOWLY the years creep by,
  Since thou art gone;
 Around me shadows lie,
 And I'm alone.

A fragment of a hymn—
  A braid of hair—
A portrait old and dim—
  A vacant chair,

Are all that speak to me
  This lone midnight,
Telling their tale of thee,
  Now out of sight.

Whisper thy love once more,
  Nor silent be;
Send from that fadeless shore
  Love's blessing free.

Come back, bright days, long dead—
  Come back again!
Return, O joys that fled,
  And ease my pain!

But why this anxious plea?—
  'Tis vain indeed;
For by fate's stern decree
  This heart must bleed.

The Deserted Castle.

GRIM and gray are the castle walls
    That overlook Mendota lake;
  No sounds float thro' the stately halls
Where once the merry feasters spake.

'Tis many years since life and thought
  Were active at this cheerless hearth;
Now all is vacancy, and naught
  Is seen of past, forgotten mirth.

The proud escutcheon still remains
  Above the weather-beaten door;
But from the turret belfry strains
  Will gladly echo nevermore.

The castle's chambers once were filled
   With light, and love, and dazzling throngs,
And happy, youthful hearts were thrilled
   With harp's wild thrum and grand old songs.

But broken are those harp-strings now ;
   The songs of yore have died away ;
Nor longer glows the dancer's brow,
   So radiant in a by-gone day.

Chill winds sweep thro' the naked rooms
   And sigh in lobbies dark and lone,
As mourners sigh among the tombs
   When weeping for the dead and gone.

No more will welcome voices speak
   Within those crumbling castle walls;
No more will festive music break
   The stillness of its solemn halls.

'Tis now the haunt of robbers bold,
   Who thread its courts when day is done,
Their tales of plunder to unfold
   In a perfidious undertone.

Then, turn aside ; no longer stay
   Where gloom and desolation fright ;
Let phantom guests glide in to play
   And feast within those halls to-night.

The Voice of Song.

SING me a song when I'm lonely—
  A heartfelt and soul-stirring lay;
  For a tender ballad only
Can comfort and never betray.

Sing softly when I am weary
  With cares that corrode and annoy;
And e'en if the day be dreary,
  Your ballad shall fill me with joy.

Sing sweetly when woe and sadness
  Cast o'er me their shadows so deep;
Your sonnet shall bring me gladness,
  And lovingly soothe me to sleep.

Sing when my earthly hopes perish,
  And clouds of misfortune affright,
And the lovely things I cherish
  ·Fade forever out of my sight.

And when I draw near the river,
　Whose waters are sullen and cold,
O sing of that bright forever
　And the beautiful city of gold!

Then as I pass through the portal
　That leads to the home of the blest,
Celestial anthems immortal
　Shall bring to me infinite rest.

Winter.

THE charming summer days are gone,
　And woods are pale and bare;
　The liquid notes of birds float not
Upon the darkened air.

The meadows, where my feet erst strayed,
　Are naked now and cold;
The flowers are dead—the gorgeous flowers
　That decked the open wold.

I see no more the mountain stream
　Leap blithely down the hill;
Held fast in winter's icy chains,
　That stream is dead and still.

7

The maples, that in autumn days
  Were bright in crimson dress,
Are swaying now before the blast
  In gloomy nakedness.

To human life death's winter comes,
  When fairest flowers must fade;
And in the cold, relentless grave
  Our darling ones are laid.

But as the flowerets re-appear
  When falls the April rain,
So, in the future, we shall find
  The loved and lost again.

The Legend of the Beautiful Hand.

THREE maidens once had a dispute
    About the beauty of their hands;
  One dipped her hand into a stream,
Then said, " I care not in what lands
You roam, you'll find in royal line
No hand more beautiful than mine."

Another maiden quickly plucked
    Some fruit, until her hand was pink;
Then she remarked, "There is no hand
    More lovely than this one, I think;
Nor is there hand of art's design
More shapely than this hand of mine."

The other gathered violets
    Until her hands were fair as flowers,
And quite as fragrant, too, as they;
    Then her sweet voice rang through the bowers:
" My hands, now full of violets blue,
Outrival all in form and hue !"

A haggard woman, passing by,
　　Paused when she reached the maidens fair,
And in a trembling voice she said :
　　" I am so poor and worn with care !
Who will have pity now on me ?
Who will show Christian charity ? "

All three denied the beggar's suit ;
　　But there was one who sat near by,
Unwashed in stream, unstained with fruit,
　　Untouched by flowerets' fragrancy,
And she had pity on the poor,
And gave her from her little store.

The beggar there and then inquired
　　As to the subject of debate,
And the three maidens showed their hands,
　　And asked the mendicant to state
Which hand of those before her face,
Had the most shapeliness and grace.

" 'Tis not the hand washed in the brook ;
　　'Tis not the hand that's tipped with red,
Nor yet the hand adorned with flowers ;
　　But 'tis the hand," the beggar said,
" That freely giveth to the poor
Who have to beg from door to door."

A change passed o'er her as she spoke ;
  Light came into her faded eyes ;
The haggard look and wrinkles fled,
  Till, as an angel from the skies,
She stood before that circle mute :—
Heav'n solved the question in dispute !

Retrospection.

DEDICATED TO MRS. W. M. COLWELL.

AS I view the little playthings
    Scattered o'er the bedroom floor,
  And behold the little carriage
That my darling wheels no more—
Ah ! what mem'ries sad and olden
  Cluster near to make me weep ;
In my sadness I remember
  When my baby fell asleep.

Years have flown since that dark morning
  When the angels bore him home
To that land of rest and gladness,
  Where no sorrows ever come ;
Yet those little toys are lying
  As he left them in his play,
And at eve I gaze upon them
  Till the daylight fades away.

How those little toys remind me
  Of the child I would embrace!
Even through the mists and darkness
  I now seem to see his face;
But that face will draw no nearer,
  Though I hail it o'er the tide;
Precious angel rests in heaven—
  Rests close by the Saviour's side.

Yet those playthings in that bedroom,
  Silent, gloomy and forlorn,
Point me back to years so blissful,
  When bereavement's cruel thorn
Had not pierced into my bosom,
  All my fondest hopes to blight;
Still I'm better for my trials;
  God is near in sorrow's night.

Though my way be dark and dreary,
  And the little face I love
Beams no more upon my vision
  Like a twinkling star above,
I am patiently awaiting
  For the coming of that time
When I'll greet my angel baby
  In that far off, heavenly clime.

To-Day.

TO-DAY is yours. The work you have to do
 Must speedily be done;
  The night is coming when man's task is through;
 Soon sets the shining sun.

To-day is the auspicious time for zeal
 To show itself in deeds
Sublime. Begin your work for others' weal,
 And go where honor leads.

If you would reach the heights of fair renown,
 You must advance to-day;
On you the solemn night will soon come down;
 Then labor while you may.

This hour your fortitude is to be tried;
 Show, then, your power to bear
The fierce assaults of sin that, far and wide,
 The young and old ensnare.

Thy future weal or failure will depend
  On purposes that now
Are hidden in thy youthful mind.   They send
  Defeat or crown the brow

With honor's dazzling and unfading wreath;
  So live this present day,
That good men shall extol thy deeds and breathe
  Thy name with ecstasy.

Rest in the Grave.

I LONG to be laid in the silent grave;
  I am weary with toil and care;
    And 'tis rest, sweet rest, that I fondly crave,
  For life's burdens are hard to bear.

I long to be laid 'neath the daisies white;—
  The flowers are kind watchers, you know;—
Then I'd nevermore dread the cheerless night,
  And my tears would nevermore flow.

I long to repose 'neath the willows' shade,
  With my hands folded on my breast,
And to sleep the dreamless sleep of the dead,
  For I'm weary and sigh for rest.

I long to be laid in my narrow bed,
   As a child, that is tired of play,
Is soothed to sleep when his prayer has been said
   And night's curtains have shut out the day.

I long to depart from the sorrow and strife,
   And go where my eyes would not weep,
And lay down, for aye, the burdens of life,
   And be resting in dreamless sleep.

Unnoticed.

THERE is many a faithful toiler
   Who receives not a word of praise,
  To gladden his heart in the struggle
  And illuminate life's dark maze.

One encouraging word would comfort
   That fatigued and dejected one,
Who simply desires to be noticed
  For the few good deeds he has done.

There are lonely hearts in life's pathway,
   That need commendation and cheer;
But such have to labor and suffer,
  Unacknowledged, from year to year.

They are always found in their places,
  And are faithful to every trust;
Yet they never get recognition,
  When, to honor them would be just.

Oh, deign to speak words of approval
  To the toiler noble and true!
It will lift from his heart a burden
  And revive his spirits anew.

We all like to know when our service
  Brings good to the young or the old;
A word of deserved approbation
  Fills the heart with comfort untold.

Christmas Eve.

COME, sit beside the fire to-night;
  The home and hearth are warm and bright,
    As playfully the dazzling light
  Dances about our feet;
And let us talk of olden days,
And sing once more the old-time lays
That waken cherished memories,
    So sacred and so sweet.

We'll wander back through vanished years,
Till what we love again appears;
But you must wipe away the tears
    And not look quite so sad;
For this is merry Christmas Eve;
'Tis not the proper time to grieve;
So let us all our troubles leave
    Behind, and now be glad.

Why should the heart be filled with pain,
When scenes of yore come back again,
And when we catch the sweet refrain
    Of some familiar song

That echoed out in happier hours,
When life, equipped with youthful powers,
Seemed sweeter than the summer flowers
   That blossomed all day long?

Your hair, good wife, is turning gray;
Nor is your laugh so strong and gay
As when, in years long passed away,
   I lingered by your side;
But though old age creeps on you now,
And sorrow's wrinkles mark your brow,
You seem as fair to me, I vow,
   As when you were my bride.

I know why tears suffuse your eyes;
You're thinking of the one who lies
So still beneath the wintry skies,
   Unconscious of the wind
That moans and sobs around her bed,
Or the swaying trees above her head
That keep their vigil near the dead,
   Like watchers true and kind.

I think 'tis just ten years ago
Since she, with eyes and cheeks aglow,
Sat in this chair, and charmed us so
   With her enchanting lay.

Alack! we little thought that she
So soon would leave both you and me;
It seems as though it was to be;
   I feel it every day.

Don't you recall the time, dear Nell,—
'Twas Christmas, I remember well,—
When Maud spoke words I dare not tell?
   They made you weep, I know.
She talked of death and heavenly things,
And of the songs an angel sings
In presence of the King of kings,
   Where joys forever flow.

Soon afterward her voice grew still,
And strains that made our pulses thrill
With ecstasy, no more did fill
   Our home with gladness rare.
As a sweet songster of the dell
Warbles, in autumn, his farewell,
So closed her song when dead leaves fell
   And winter chilled the air.

But let us look on life's bright side,
For this is Christmas eventide;
And let us each, whate'er betide,
   Trust in our Father God;

Let us now think of Bethlehem's child,
Who came to be a Saviour mild;
And may we, sweetly reconciled,
   Bow 'neath the chastening rod.

Each Christmas time should bring good cheer;
And though past scenes now re-appear
As we recall each vanished year,
   Let us no longer grieve.
The future may be brighter, wife,
With less of anguish, less of strife;
So let's forget the ills of life,
   And sing this Christmas Eve!

The Fleeting.

HOW fleeting are the things of earth !
  We love them but to lose them all,
  And lose them, too, beyond recall,
Though cherished for their priceless worth.

The garden rose that blossomed in
  The mild, delightful summer day,
  Has long since faded quite away,
And with it all its gentle kin.

I love the soft blue summer skies ;
  But winter's clouds have hid that blue
  From sight ; and tender grass that grew
In flow'ry vales, now frozen lies.

My childhood's home, so dear to me,
  Is now no more.   The loved are gone,
  And through the world I walk alone,
With nothing left but memory.

THE FLEETING.

The years have flown on noiseless wing,
  And radiant, blissful days of yore
  Will come to cheer me nevermore;
Yet they are worth remembering.

I had a friend—a friend most dear!
  Who made my earth-life glad and bright;
  But from his eyes fled love's warm light,
And now my path is lone and drear.

My heart is reaching out in vain
  For that to which it might aye cling:
  Ah! earthly joys are vanishing;
This life is full of loss and pain.

But hope, sad heart! To thee is given
  The promise of a future home,
  Where disappointments never come,
And that unclouded home is Heaven.

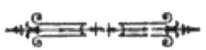

Befriendment.

IN life's journey we are climbing,
    And how oft our strength departs!
  But 'tis sweet to get assistance
From true, sympathetic hearts.

O how many daily perish
    For the want of needed aid!
O the souls that, crushed and sorrowing,
    Move through life uncheered, dismayed!

Tempted, wounded, struggling mortals
    Are around us everywhere;
In life's battle they are falling,
    And are dying in despair.

We can cheer them, if we're willing,
    With a loving word or deed;
And our kindly aid will help them
    To push onward and succeed.

8

Let those resting on the summit
   Now reach down the friendly hand
To help upward some weak brother
   Who has scarcely strength to stand.

Such an effort will be noble ;
   It will bring a rich reward ;
For the good done to the needy
   Is good done unto the Lord.

Mother's Vacant Chair.

ONE relic in my lowly home
   I value above jewels rare ;
   Its presence makes old mem'ries bloom ;—
'Tis sainted mother's vacant chair.

I hear it, as in days long dead ;
   The sound comes to me everywhere—
The creaking noise those rockers made
   On mother's worn-out, vacant chair.

I seem to see that face so bright,
   And catch the whisper of a prayer
She breathed confidingly each night,
   When kneeling by this quaint old chair.

How often, in my early youth,
   She taught me, with an earnest air,
Deep lessons from the Book of Truth,
   While sitting in this easy chair!

Alas! her voice grew faint one day,
   And in my heart arose despair;
Closing her dim eyes peacefully,
   She left to me this vacant chair.

To-day I touch life's minor chords;
   I sink beneath my load of care;
But still I'm cheered by tender words
   My mother spoke from this old chair.

O voices of the olden days!
   O joys that made the world so fair!
O sweet, delightful memories
   That cluster round this vacant chair!

Whatever change the years have wrought,
   Yet ever shines Hope's splendent star;
And in my prayer oft comes the thought:
   In Heav'n there is no vacant chair.

The Bright Side.

EARTH-life has its lights and its shades,
    And 'tis true that each rose has its thorn;
  Yet how oft, when a fond hope fades,
We discern but the night—not the morn.

When fair summer flowers lie down
  To repose 'neath the mantle of snow,
At that very moment we frown
  And our hopes and our pleasures forego.

When stars disappear from our sky
  And the shadows fall thick on life's road,
Our hearts in deep loneliness sigh
  As we sink under sorrow's great load.

O look on the bright side of life!
  We shall yet hear the song-birds of spring;
Sweet peace will come after the strife,
  And, the weeping once over, we'll sing.

No matter how dreary the path,
  There's a flower blooming in it, we're told;
Then, blissful the thought that God hath
  For the weary built mansions of gold!

We'll cull out the joys from the woes,
  And observe the glad smiles 'mong the tears;
Nor shall our feet trample the rose,
  Though so thorny the rose-bush appears.

The Silent Soldier.

JULY, 1885.

REST, soldier, rest! Thy eventide has come;
    Sweet be thy slumber in Death's dreamless
      sleep;
  Over thy breast let cooling zephyrs creep,
Wafting the fragrance of the summer bloom.

Hushed, at this moment, is the nation's breath,
  While her loved Chieftain's body lies in state,
  Guarded and watched from early morn till late,
Within the voiceless citadel of Death.

The grateful, sobbing millions bend above
  That clay within which animation burned,
  And weep o'er him whose manful spirit spurned
Intrigue ;—whose heart was full of patriot love.

O, Appomattox hero ! on whose brow
  Of marble coldness sitteth Death, and yet
  Who liveth ;—*rest !* For thou hast bravely met
The king of foes, and thou art victor now.

Penitence.

FATHER, I'm tired and sigh for rest,
  Such rest as Thou alone canst give;
    My wounded soul, so long oppressed,
Desires the life the righteous live.

I cannot longer do without
  The saving grace that comes from Thee,
O help my faith, remove all doubt,
  Release me from captivity !

Weary of sin and crushed with grief,
  I look to Thee for solace sweet;
Then graciously impart relief
  To this poor suppliant at Thy feet.

Help me to rise in manhood's might
  And boldly strive to conquer sin ;
In the momentous moral fight
  I want Thine aid that I may win.

Speak now and bid my fears subside ;
  Lighten the burden that I bear ;
Then shall I in Thy love abide,
  And know the worth of fervent prayer.

Easter Hymn.

HAIL to the risen Lord,
    Who triumphed over death !
  As King He is adored
With heaven's united breath.

From the dark vault He came,
  Shining with heav'nly light ;
Let earth's hosts laud His name
  With reverential might.

Angelic voices swell
  In loud, exultant strains,
For Christ has conquered hell,
  And He triumphant reigns.

Death's dismal night has now
    A resurrection morn;
Then, glow each heart and brow:
    Immortal life is born!

May we in Christ now live,
    Partakers of His grace,
And in His service strive,
    Till we shall see His face.

Greatness.

I WATCHED a grand procession moving by;
    No poor were in the funeral train;
No tears were shed.   I heard no mourner's cry
    Commingling with the minor strain.

Surely, said I, some good man goes to rest;
    For such a brilliant pageantry
Would never honor one who had oppressed
    The poor with acts of cruelty.

Another funeral train I soon descried,
    Unlike the first that passed along;
The while I gazed I saw but little pride
    Or pomp among the solemn throng.

There were a thousand faces wet with tears;
  And grateful people of all creeds,
On looking backward over by-gone years,
  Recalled the dead man's gen'rous deeds.

The humble poor pressed near the open grave
  To pay their debt of gratitude
To him who sympathized with men and gave
  The needy aid, the hungry food.

Who was the greater man? I said at last—
  The one whose death drew not a tear?
Or he whose flight a sombrous shadow cast
  Over the weary strugglers here?

A moment's pause, and then the answer came:
  Remember, he alone is great
Whose sympathy, like an increasing flame,
  Consumes all selfishness and hate.

Tired.

I WOULD lie down and take the needed rest
 After fatiguing toil ;
 But when I think of hearts that are unblest,
  I from such rest recoil.

For who but selfish mortals could behold
  The vanquished in this life,
And ne'er desire to help both young and old
  To conquer in the strife.

I sometimes tire of singing o'er again
  The song of sympathy ;
But when sad hearts are gladdened by the strain
  I cannot silent be.

Tired of the world, I often long to shrink
  Back into solitude ;
For such a calm, secluded life, I think,
  Would seem so sweet, so good.

Yet when I but reflect on all the wrong,
    The tumult and the fears
In human life, I deeply mourn, and long
    To comfort those in tears.

So, though I'm weary, I will not lie down
    Till my life-work is done;
And then I know that God will give a crown
    After the race is run.

The rest will be the sweeter by-and-by,
    If I toil on and wait;
And though I weep, my tears will all be dry
    When I pass through heaven's gate.

My joy will be the greater, too, I know,
    If I but do my best
To lighten weary burdens here below
    And bring to others rest.

The Fisherman.

HOME from his toil a fisher goes
    When the long day begins to close;
    Light is his heart and bright his brow
As laughing children greet him now;
And his rude cottage, filled with mirth,
Is just the happiest place on earth.

The evening shadows once more come;
But never fisher's boat sails home,
And the tired mother drops a tear,
For her faint heart is seized with fear,
And children's eyes look wistfully
Far out upon the moaning sea.

The waves break wildly on the strand;
Dense darkness covers sea and land;
Still higher the huge breakers rise!
Still darker grow the cruel skies!
O mighty God! protect and save
That fisher from an ocean grave.

When the long-looked-for morning **came**,
All decked in robes of light and flame,
The watchers spied upon the sand
A boat that drifted **to** the land,
And weary hearts by that **sea** shore
Shall **mourn** for him who comes no more.

Duty.

 ISCHARGE thy duty, come what may ;
    Work through the golden hours of day,
      For night approaches rapidly.

No matter if the world does frown,
Lay not thy mighty weapons down ;
Go, bear the cross and win the crown !

Live for a purpose grand and true ;
Keep God and heaven in thy view,
Nor fear the gloom thou passest through.

Watch o'er the children as they glide
Here and there on life's sunny side ;
Be thou their tender and loving guide.

If thou wouldst make thine own heart sing,
Then, to the hearts in sorrow, bring
The sweets of love's rich offering.

Duty, well done, brings happiness;
And man's true wealth in the world of bliss
Is simply the good he does in this.

God Understands.

I HAVE not much to offer
    When I go to God in prayer,
  And yet I know He loves me
  And keeps me in His care.

Nor can I, in my weakness,
    Do all I wish to do;
  But, then, my Father pities
    And understands me, too.

Sometimes I feel so weary,
    Sometimes my faith is small;
  Yet why should I be downcast?
    God understands it all.

He knows of my besetments,
  My sorrows and my fears,
And sympathizes with me
  When my eyes are filled with tears.

Though I am weak and sinful,
  And often err or stray,
My frailties he considers
  With tenderness each day.

Worthless are my thanksgivings
  And offerings, I ween;
But He will not despise them—
  He knoweth what I mean.

He understands my blindness,
  As all His dealing shows;
So if I blunder often,
  He knows the cause—He knows.

And though I am not perfect,
  I thrust my hand in His,
Willing to walk beside Him
  Who knows just how it is.

Beyond.

YOU wonder when I say I fear not death ;
    But when at last I draw the parting breath,
    And I am ushered into the unknown,
I shall not feel that I am quite alone ;
For will there not be near me those I knew
And loved—friends who, long years ago, withdrew
From all terrestrial things and sensuous life,
Never again to wrestle in earth's strife ?
Will not the countless dead be everywhere
About me in that other state, to share
My deep remorse or ecstasy of bliss,
Just as friends greet us in a world like this ?
Methinks I shall not be alone when o'er
Death's stream I pass and touch that unknown shore :
I shall but join a grand, majestic throng,
Outnumb'ring all that to this sphere belong ;
And none, among the armies of the dead,
Feel lonely 'mid the silence deep and dread.

The Heart's Springtime.

WHAT joy comes to the heart in spring,
    When the first notes of robins ring
    In gladness on the April air,
Filling the woods—long pale, and bare,
And voiceless—with loud symphonies
That echo the Creator's praise!

Each life must have its winter time,
When songs of melody sublime
Give place to plaintive airs that fill
The human heart with fears of ill;
But winter does not always stay,
To mock at us in cruelty.

As Nature's sober realms put on
Bright robes when wintry days are gone,
So in the human heart, long sad—
Long in the garb of mourning clad—
Spring bright, fresh flowers of Hope and Peace
When winter's wailful sonnets cease.

9

The Lessons Flowers Teach.

FLOWERETS beautiful and bright!
　　Voiceless ye are, and yet
　Ye teach such lessons day and night
We never can forget.

Ye tell us of God's boundless love
　With silent eloquence;
Ye bid us onward, upward move
　In faith and confidence.

Ye cheer the faint and heavy heart
　Upon life's weary way,
And when affliction's tear-drops start
　Ye smile those tears away.

In the enchanting realm of flowers
　We nobler grow in thought,
Till all our better, higher powers
　With virtue are inwrought.

Seeing the lilies how they grow
  Beneath God's special care,
We learn to trust Him and to go
  Before His throne in **prayer.**

O flowers! your voiceless lips to all
  Lessons of love impart;
They whisper hope when faith is small
  And sorrow fills the heart.

Darker would be this world of ours
  And more mysterious,
Without the star-eyed, golden flowers
  That bloom to comfort us.

Bloom on! O flowerets sweet and gay!
  Emblems of hope and love,
Emblems of resurrection day,
  And of our home above.

A War Memory.

HARK! the muffled drum is beating, ere the sun
    has mounted high,
    And away in yonder distance I can hear the
bugle's cry.

I can see the mute procession moving gracefully along
To pay homage to those heroes who fell fighting 'gainst
    the wrong.

Here, my child, I wish to linger, on this Decoration
    morn—
Here within this silent city that knows neither pride
    nor scorn;

And I'll tell to you a story that will cause the tears
    to flow,
Of a fierce and mighty contest that took place long
    years ago.

In that flow'ry grave, so near you, sleeps my brother
brave and true;
He was wounded in the battle—he who wore the coat
of blue.

We both marched away together when the call from
Lincoln came;
Side-by-side we both contended to defend our country's
name.

Mother wept to see us leaving the old home we both
held dear;
And though to manhood we had risen, *we* scarce could
hide the tear.

'Twas at Perryville that Wilford got his fatal wound
and fell;
I was by his side that moment—in the midst of shot
and shell.

Then I bore him from the carnage and the thickest of
the fight,
And I tried to check his fever through that long and
fearful night.

But his heated breath grew fainter, ay, and paler grew
his cheek;
And before his pulse-beats ended, these sad words I
heard him speak:

'Brother, I am faint—I'm dying—dying ere I hear
   the shout
Of my country's glorious triumph; I am surely mus-
   tered out!

"But I have discharged my duty to my God and
   native land,
And I do not dread the future while the Captain holds
   my hand.

"But I thought I'd march home with you when the
   strifes of war should cease,
And unite with all my comrades in the thrilling song
   of Peace!

"Ah, this cherished hope is blasted! yet I'll die a
   soldier brave,
And you'll wrap the flag around me—the old flag I
   fought to save!

"In the springtime fragrant roses o'er my lonely grave
   will bloom,
And loved voices will oft whisper kind words of me at
   my tomb.

"But I ne'er shall see the flow'rets, nor shall I ever
   hear
The sweet, familiar voices that allured my youthful
   ear.

" I shall ne'er behold the homestead where together
    we have played—
Never gaze upon the mountain, nor stroll through the
    the wooded glade.

" I shall never hear the robins singing in the old oak
    tree
That **in scorching** days of summer often sheltered you
    and me.

" **Oh, I feel so cold and weary ! and earth's** scenes fade
    from my sight ;
But it's **glorious, Brother** Charley, to die **knowing** all
    is right !

" **I can hear sweet music stealing o'er the** waters dark
    and chill ;
I can see a gorgeous city **on a** sun-illumined hill.

" **And I'll** soon pass **through the portals of that gate
    of purest gold—**
Soon **be free from earthly anguish and** rejoice with
    bliss untold.

" **Tell kind mother** not to sorrow over her departed boy,
For I'm **going to a** country where are found true peace
    and joy.

"Now her blessing rests upon me, and she prays for
    me and all ;—
Then, a last farewell! dear brother, for I hear the
    bugle-call!"

This, my child, will end the story I intended to relate;
For I see the long procession passing through the
    graveyard gate.

Let us place this wreath of blossoms just above dear
    Wilford's breast ;
It will show that we still love him as he sleeps in
    dreamless rest.

Then we'll go, in tearful silence, from this city of the
    slain,
And await the Resurrection, when the dead shall live
    again.

Life's Problem.

I.

A ROSY morn and a cloudless sky ;
   Hope in the heart ;
      No tear-drops start ;
Never a pain and never a sigh.

II.

A child's sweet laugh, and its little kiss
   Upon the cheek,
      And voices speak
In tend'rest tones, and there's nought but bliss.

III.

Then come distress and corroding care ;
   The joy has gone,
      The face is wan,
And there is an agonizing prayer.

IV.

Blue eyes are closed, and the child's sweet hymn
   Is heard no more
      On earth's dark shore,
And a mother weeps till her eyes are dim.

10

V.

Then mem'ry calls back the long ago,
    And hair grows gray,
    While shadows play
Long after the autumn evening's glow.

VI.

Folded the hands, and ended the strife
    Of weary years;
    Dried are the tears;
Thus closes the scene;—and such is life!

When I am Dead.

WHEN I am dead, will you draw gently near
My corse, and shed o'er it a heartfelt tear?
Will you bring sweet forget-me-nots to lay
Upon my breast when I am laid away?

Will you in fondness press your warm, soft hand
Against my brow, when to the spirit land
I've passed? Or will you heedlessly go by,
Nor pause to look on me with tearful eye?

Will you neglect me in that solemn hour,
When my frail life resigns her present power?
You loved me dearly in the days of yore,
And eulogized my graces o'er and o'er.

My sins you oft condoned with spirit free,
And when I erred you showed me charity;
Ah! will you be as kind when I have sped
Beyond earth's shores and joined the silent dead?

Will you come softly near my resting place,
And there recall to mind my form and face—
The rhymes I penned—the songs I used to sing
In good old days well worth remembering?

Perchance when death releases me from pain
You will not fondly think of me again;
But should you plant no flower above my breast
Your cold neglect will not disturb my rest!

www.ingramcontent.com/pod-product-compliance
Lightning Source LLC
Chambersburg PA
CBHW020750020726
47495CB00008B/2368